Shacquan Robinson

WHAT HAPPENED TO US

The Missing 5 C's of a
Relationship

Umbrella Dynasty Publishing

"What Happened To Us"

The Missing 5 C's of a Relationship

SHACQUAN C. ROBINSON

Dedication

...to that special woman...

Table of Contents

Really?

To the left to the left,
We really let mainstream media tell us how to love the next
We stopped seeking advice through generational blessings
and started seeking advice through lies deceit and finessing

To one up on the next person in fear of getting our hearts
crushed
No one does nice things or talks about things previously
discussed
One small argument we run to social media
Options and opinions from others, sex with randoms now
chlamydia

Only dating cuz we like liquor and weed
Forgetting that peace, structure and love is what we need
Mix one tribe with another to create a nation
But society has tainting our minds leading to family
assassination

We're supposed to be the staple of moral values
Black people get it together let's kill relationship abuse
I'm biblically grounded when it comes to relationships
My next will be my last I hope it clicks

Please Understand where I'm coming from
Love is really what we need to overcome

Shacquan Robinson, written January 25, 2023 at 6:40am

Introduction

A lot of us were raised by single parent homes. And for some, the benefit of two parent homes helped jumpstart us into a successful life, especially when it comes to relationships. We got to see love from both sexes and how they express it.

It's sad to say that nowadays that is not prevalent anymore. But the blame is not solely on the lack of both parents. It comes from multiple negative sources. Most pushed out by miserable misinformation throughout our society. We really decided to take advice from podcasters who ain't seen nothing in life except reality tv shows. It's damaging our mental health now most of us are fucked up.

I want to help fix the problem, not recite the same bullshit over and over. I'm bringing you first hand knowledge from being married and divorced. Knowledge handed to me from successful marriages and pimps. From my mom and my dad. From my grandparents and uncles.

Black people let's bring healthy relationships back into our culture.

"A good Woman is an investment. A good Man is a gift. But a good Relationship is the foundation to success."

~ Shacquan Robinson

"What Happened To Us"

The Missing 5 C's of A Relationship

Part I

Understanding Love

Understanding love is a complex and subjective topic, as it can mean different things to different people. What people don't realize is that some people are struggling with love in this generation because they are healed, they know what they want. They speak highly and do high vibrational things.

On the other hand, the connections to certain people fail because most relationships today are only rooted in trauma bonds. When one person is not held in slavery by those bonds but the other is, it brings an issue of inequality to the relationship. Or what most say, unequally yoked. Meaning they start having issues, problems and situations that cause the breakup. Then you have people who feed off trauma bonds and they're relationships last longer because they're toxic for each other. Which isn't healthy at all. Longer doesn't mean successful.

Those who choose peace and real love over trauma will have difficulty in relationships because most people that we meet are emotionally damaged and they don't want to fix it. They definitely know how, they just won't put in the work, making it difficult or challenging for their person or other people. They tend to cling to the things that are bad for them while fighting the things that are good. Healed people seek healthy connections.

The Washington Post made an article that stated that 60% percent of the unmarried couples who had been together for less than 2 months were no longer together after 1 year of a study group conducted. I believe about 70% of the relationships that we see are actually trauma bonds, the ones that end quickly or even the ones that last. I say relationships are needed, but some of those involved in that game "need" the other person to make them feel whole because they're both mentally, emotionally and/or spiritually destroyed.

It's ways we can combat the destruction of the relationship and potential family dynamics. Avoid toxic behaviors and trauma related connections that take us nowhere but to depression and/or the mental if not physical graveyard.

Here are five quick ways to gain a deeper understanding of love:

Self-reflection and introspection

Start by reflecting on your own experiences and feelings of love. Ask yourself what love means to you, how it feels, and what it looks like in your life. Consider your past relationships, both romantic and non-romantic, and analyze the emotions and actions associated with love. Self-reflection can help you gain insights into your own understanding of love and how it manifests in your life.

Study different theories & perspectives

Love has been a subject of study and contemplation for centuries. Explore different theories and perspectives on love from various disciplines such as psychology, philosophy, sociology, and literature. Read books, articles, and research papers that delve into the nature of love, its different forms, and the factors that influence it. Understanding different theories can broaden your perspective and provide you with a more comprehensive understanding of love.

Seek wisdom from others

Engage in conversations with people who have experienced love in different ways. Talk to friends, family members, mentors, or even therapists about their experiences and insights on love. Listen to their stories, advice, and perspectives, and try to understand how love has impacted their lives. Hearing different perspectives can help you gain a more nuanced understanding of love and its complexities.

Practice empathy & compassion

Love is often associated with empathy and compassion. To understand love better, practice putting yourself in others' shoes and try to understand their experiences and emotions. Cultivate empathy by actively listening to others, being open-minded, and showing compassion towards their struggles and joys. By developing empathy, you can gain a deeper understanding of the emotions and connections that love fosters.

Embrace personal growth and self-love

Love starts from within. To understand love fully, it is essential to cultivate self-love and engage in personal growth. Take time to explore your own needs, desires, and boundaries. Practice self-care, self-compassion, and self-acceptance. By nurturing a healthy relationship with yourself, you can develop a stronger foundation for understanding and experiencing love in your relationships with others.

Remember that understanding love is an ongoing journey, and it may evolve and change over time. It is a deeply personal and subjective experience, and everyone's understanding of love may differ. Embrace the process of exploration and learning, and be open to new perspectives and insights along the way.

Now let's get to the meat and potatoes. Talk about what's missing in relationships that actually make them grow exponentially. We as a generation lack these things and that is why relationships fail. Only lasting 3 months, 6 months barely a year. No discipline and no real skills to manage the relationships. But I'm going to break down what I know and what we all can do to keep relationships long, successful and healthy like our parents and grandparents.

Welcome to What Happened to Us? - The Missing 5 C's of a Relationship

Part II

The 5 C's

The 5 C's are a list of qualities I believe every relationship should have. It is inspired by the help of one of my OG's. A good relationship is characterized by several key qualities that contribute to its strength and longevity. These qualities include trust, communication, respect, support, and compromise. But not limited to those. In fact I will speak five I really believe in the most.

Trust is the foundation of any healthy relationship. It involves having confidence in your partner's honesty, reliability, and intentions. Trust allows individuals to feel secure and safe in the relationship, fostering a sense of emotional intimacy.

A good relationship is important for several reasons. Firstly, it provides emotional support and companionship, enhancing overall well-being and happiness. It creates a sense of belonging and security, reducing stress and anxiety. A healthy relationship also promotes personal growth and self-improvement, as partners can learn from each other's strengths and weaknesses.

Furthermore, a good relationship serves as a source of motivation and encouragement. It can inspire individuals to achieve their goals and pursue their dreams. Having a supportive partner can boost self-confidence and provide a sense of purpose and fulfillment.

I strongly believe that a good relationship contributes to a healthy and stable society. Strong relationships serve as role models for others, promoting positive relationship dynamics and values. They also provide a nurturing environment for children, fostering their emotional development and teaching them important life skills.

In conclusion, a good relationship is important for personal happiness, growth, and well-being, as well as for the overall health of society.

Chapter I

Commitment

Commitment is a crucial aspect of any successful relationship. It shows that you are fully invested in your partner and willing to put in the effort to make the relationship work. Commitment is related to support and is crucial in a good relationship. It involves being there for each other during both the ups and downs of life. Supporting each other emotionally, mentally, and physically helps to build a strong bond and fosters a sense of teamwork and partnership. Here are a few pieces of advice to help you navigate commitment in your relationship:

1. Communicate openly: Talk to your partner about your expectations and desires in terms of commitment. Make sure you're on the same page and willing to work towards a common goal.

2. Be reliable and consistent: Show up for your partner consistently, both in small and big ways. Being reliable and dependable will make your partner feel secure and valued.

3. Prioritize the relationship: Commitment means making your relationship a priority in your life. This may involve making sacrifices, compromising, and dedicating time and effort to nurturing the relationship.

4. Embrace vulnerability: Being committed means being vulnerable with your partner. Allow yourself to open up emotionally, share your fears, hopes, and dreams. This vulnerability will deepen your connection and build trust.

5. Stay true to your word: Follow through on your promises and commitments. If you make a commitment to your partner, honor it. This builds trust and shows that you are reliable.

6. Support each other's growth: Encourage your partner to pursue their goals and dreams, and be there to support them. A committed relationship is about helping each other grow and become the best versions of yourselves.

7. Be willing to work through challenges: Commitment means being willing to work through challenges and conflicts. Relationships aren't always easy, but a committed couple is willing to put in the effort to overcome obstacles together.

Remember, commitment is a choice you make every day. It's about being there for your partner, showing up, and actively choosing to love and support each other.

Chapter II

Compromise

Relationships require compromise in order to thrive and grow. Compromising is the ability to find common ground and make decisions that satisfy both partners' needs. It requires flexibility, understanding, and a willingness to find solutions that benefit the relationship as a whole. Compromise helps to avoid power imbalances and promotes fairness and equality. Here are a few pieces of advice on how to navigate the art of compromise:

1. Communication is key: Open and honest communication is the foundation of a healthy relationship. Discuss your needs, desires, and concerns with your partner. By understanding each other's perspectives, you can find common ground and make compromises that satisfy both of you.

2. Seek win-win solutions: When faced with a disagreement, aim for solutions that benefit both parties. Look for compromises where both individuals feel heard and valued. This not only ensures a fair outcome but also strengthens the bond between you.

3. Choose your battles wisely: Not every disagreement needs to be resolved with compromise. It's important to prioritize which issues are truly significant and which can be let go. By focusing on the important matters, you can

avoid unnecessary conflicts and save your energy for the compromises that truly matter.

4. Find middle ground: Compromise often involves finding a middle ground that satisfies both partners. Explore alternative options and be willing to meet each other halfway. This way, both individuals feel like their needs are being considered and respected.

5. Flexibility and adaptability: Relationships require flexibility and adaptability. Be open to change and willing to adjust your expectations. Remember that compromise is a two-way street, and both partners should be willing to make adjustments for the sake of the relationship.

6. Embrace creativity: Sometimes, compromise requires thinking outside the box. Get creative and brainstorm solutions that may not be obvious at first. By exploring different possibilities, you may find compromises that exceed your initial expectations.

7. Patience and empathy: Compromise takes time and effort. Be patient with each other and practice empathy. Understand that your partner may have different needs and perspectives, and be willing to step into their shoes to better understand their point of view.

Remember, compromising is a sign of strength and a willingness to prioritize the relationship. By approaching disagreements with open mindedness, respect, and a willingness to find common ground, you can build a stronger and more fulfilling partnership.

Chapter III

Communication

Effective communication is the cornerstone of any healthy and thriving relationship. Communication is vital for understanding each other's needs, desires, and concerns. Effective communication involves active listening, expressing oneself honestly and respectfully, and being open to feedback. It helps to resolve conflicts, prevent misunderstandings, and build a deeper connection. Here are some tips to help improve communication with your partner:

1. Active listening: Truly listening to your partner is crucial. Give them your full attention, maintain eye contact, and show genuine interest in what they have to say. Avoid interrupting or formulating a response before they finish speaking. By actively listening, you demonstrate respect and create a safe space for open dialogue.

2. Use "I" statements: When expressing your thoughts or feelings, use "I" statements instead of "you" statements. This helps you take responsibility for your emotions and avoids blaming or accusing your partner. For example, saying "I feel hurt when this happens" invites understanding and empathy, while saying "You always do this" can come across as confrontational.

3. Be honest and transparent: Honesty is essential for building trust in a relationship. Express yourself openly and honestly, even if it means discussing difficult or uncomfortable topics. Avoid withholding information or resorting to passive-aggressive behavior. Instead, strive for transparency and a willingness to address issues head-on.

4. Nonverbal communication: Communication is not only about words, but also about nonverbal cues. Pay attention to your body language, facial expressions, and tone of voice. Similarly, be attuned to your partner's nonverbal signals, as they often provide insights into their emotions and thoughts. By aligning your nonverbal communication with your words, you can foster better understanding and connection.

5. Timing is key: Choose the right time and place for important conversations. Avoid discussing sensitive topics when you or your partner are tired, stressed, or distracted. Find a calm and neutral environment where you both feel comfortable. By considering timing, you create a conducive atmosphere for effective communication and problem-solving.

6. Practice empathy: Empathy is the ability to understand and share the feelings of another

person. Put yourself in your partner's shoes and try to see things from their perspective. This helps foster understanding, compassion, and a deeper connection. Validating your partner's emotions and experiences can go a long way in improving communication and resolving conflicts.

7. Seek professional help when needed: If you find that communication is consistently challenging or that you and your partner are struggling to effectively communicate, don't hesitate to seek professional help. Couples therapy or counseling can provide valuable guidance and support in improving your communication skills and strengthening your relationship.

8. Pairing Words: When speaking positively about your relationship, include pairing words/subjective pronouns such as "we and us". You are one, stop thinking you're separate individuals when it's about communication. Two separate brains but the thoughts have to be in unison. It's actually quite simple when you know exactly how to communicate thoughts, opinions and point of views. Don't limit or hinder yourself just because you can't speak your peace/piece thoroughly.

9. Effective communication: While communication is essential in any relationship, effective communication can be lacking. With the

prevalence of digital communication, misunderstandings can occur due to the lack of non-verbal cues and tone. Taking the time to have open and honest conversations, actively listening to each other, and practicing empathy can help bridge this gap.

Remember, good communication requires effort, patience, and a genuine desire to overstand and be overstood. By actively practicing these tips, you can build a foundation of trust, respect, honor and intimacy in your relationship. In that way nothing will be able to break it.

Chapter IV

Christ

Yes I said it. Christ. Religion itself. My

favorite point. People in my generation believe in rocks, crystals and tree roots more than they believe in a higher creation power. To me it doesn't matter which invisible deity religion you practice. But believe in something bigger than you that guides your external judgements. I myself believe in the power of Yahweh, through his son Yashua - Yahawah Bahasham Yahawashi. Building a relationship centered around Christ can be a beautiful and enriching experience. Here are some tips to help you cultivate a Christ-centered relationship:

1. Pray together: Prayer is a powerful tool that can bring you closer to God and each other. Make it a habit to pray together as a couple, seeking guidance, strength, and blessings. Praying together allows you to share your hopes, fears, and desires with God, deepening your spiritual connection as a couple.

2. Study the Bible together: Engaging in regular Bible study as a couple can help you grow closer to Christ and understand His teachings. Choose a passage or topic that resonates with both of you and explore it together. Discussing

scripture can lead to meaningful conversations, insights, and a shared spiritual journey.

3. Attend church and worship together: Actively participating in church services and worshiping together can foster a sense of unity and shared faith. Attend church services, join Bible study groups, and engage in community service activities as a couple. These experiences will help strengthen your relationship with Christ and with each other.

4. Practice forgiveness and grace: Just as Christ forgives us, it is important to extend forgiveness and grace to your partner. Mistakes and conflicts are inevitable in any relationship, but learning to forgive and extend grace allows for healing and growth. Emulating Christ's love and forgiveness will create an atmosphere of acceptance and understanding.

5. Serve and love others: Following Christ's example, prioritize serving and loving others as a couple. Find ways to give back to your community, volunteer together, and show kindness and compassion to those in need. By

serving others, you not only honor Christ but also deepen your bond as a couple.

6. Communicate openly and honestly: Communication is key in any relationship, including your relationship with Christ. Foster open and honest communication with each other about your faith, doubts, struggles, and spiritual journey. Share your thoughts, questions, and insights, and support each other in your individual walks with Christ.

7. Trust in God's plan: Remember that your relationship is part of God's plan for your lives. Trust in His guidance and timing, and surrender any anxieties or worries to Him. Keep your focus on Christ and seek His will in your relationship. Trusting in God's plan will bring you peace and assurance as you navigate the ups and downs of life together.

Ultimately, a Christ-centered relationship is grounded in love, faith, and a shared commitment to follow YHWH's teachings. By prioritizing your relationship with Christ, you can build a strong foundation that will sustain and enrich your partnership for years to come.

Chapter V

Consistency

*C*onsistency is a crucial element in building and maintaining healthy relationships. Consistency is crucial in a relationship as it establishes a sense of stability, reliability, and trust between partners. Here are some relationship advice tips centered around consistency:

1. Be reliable: Show up for your loved ones consistently, both in good times and bad. Be reliable and dependable, so they know they can count on you. This builds trust and strengthens the bond between you.

2. Communicate regularly: Consistent communication is vital for any relationship. Make an effort to check in with your loved ones regularly, whether it's through phone calls, texts, or in-person conversations. Regular communication helps you stay connected and aware of each other's needs.

3. Follow through on your commitments: When you make promises or commitments, it's important to follow through. Consistently meeting your obligations shows that you take

your relationships seriously and that you value the trust others place in you.

4. Show up emotionally: Emotional consistency is key in relationships. Be present, empathetic, and supportive. Your loved ones should feel that you are consistently available to listen, offer advice, or simply provide a shoulder to lean on.

5. Be consistent in your actions: Your words and actions should align consistently. Being true to your values and consistently acting in ways that reflect those values helps build trust and fosters a sense of security within your relationships.

6. Prioritize quality time: Consistency in spending quality time with your loved ones is essential. Set aside dedicated time to connect, engage, and create meaningful memories together. This allows you to nurture your relationships and strengthen the bonds you share.

7. Be patient and understanding: Consistency doesn't mean perfection. It's important to be patient and understanding when mistakes

happen or when someone falls short. Offer forgiveness and work through challenges together, maintaining a consistent attitude of love and support.

Remember, consistency is not about being rigid or inflexible. It's about showing up, being present, and demonstrating that you care consistently over time. By prioritizing consistency in your relationships, you can foster trust, deepen connections, and build a strong foundation of love and support.

Like the OG said, "Be consistent with the first four!"

FINAL THOUGHTS

In today's fast-paced world, there are a few elements that may be missing in some relationships. The 5 C's are crucial in order to keep a relationship growing. But we also must remember other common elements to sustain them as well.

Quality time which is being eaten away with the rise of technology and busy schedules, quality time spent together can often be compromised. Many relationships lack dedicated time for deep conversations, shared experiences, and simply enjoying each other's company without distractions. It's important to prioritize and make time for meaningful interactions.

Emotional intimacy in the quest for convenience and efficiency, emotional intimacy can sometimes be overlooked. Building emotional connections takes time, vulnerability, and effort. It involves sharing fears, dreams, and innermost thoughts. Cultivating emotional intimacy helps create a strong foundation and deeper understanding in relationships. Mutual support in today's individualistic society, the concept of mutual support can sometimes be overshadowed. Relationships thrive when both partners feel supported and encouraged by each other. It's important to be there for each other, celebrate successes, and provide comfort during challenging times.

Prioritizing growth within each other is vital for individuals, and it also contributes to the growth of a relationship. Sometimes, relationships lack the space or encouragement for personal development. Supporting each other's goals and aspirations, and continuously working on self-improvement and growth as a couple, can help maintain a healthy and thriving relationship.

And balanced demands of work, social commitments, and personal responsibilities can often take a toll on relationships. Finding a balance between individual needs and shared time is crucial. Setting healthy boundaries and making time for self-care can help prevent burnout and ensure that both partners feel valued and fulfilled.

Remember, every relationship is unique, and what may be missing in one relationship may not be true for another. It's essential to have open and honest conversations with your partner about your needs and expectations, and to actively work on addressing any areas that may be lacking.